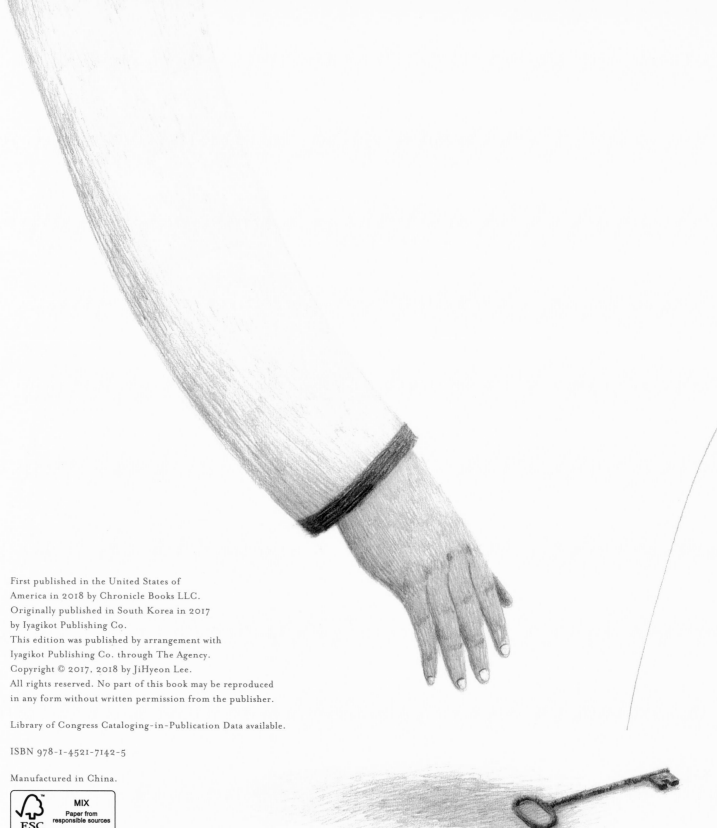

First published in the United States of
America in 2018 by Chronicle Books LLC.
Originally published in South Korea in 2017
by Iyagikot Publishing Co.
This edition was published by arrangement with
Iyagikot Publishing Co. through The Agency.
Copyright © 2017, 2018 by JiHyeon Lee.
All rights reserved. No part of this book may be reproduced
in any form without written permission from the publisher.

Library of Congress Cataloging-in-Publication Data available.

ISBN 978-1-4521-7142-5

Manufactured in China.

Design by Alice Seiler.

10 9 8 7 6 5 4

Chronicle Books LLC
680 Second Street
San Francisco, California 94107

Chronicle Books—we see things differently.
Become part of our community at www.chroniclekids.com.

DOOR

By JiHyeon Lee

chronicle books · san francisco